DANCE IN THE DESERT

DANCE IN THE

by MADELEINE L'ENGLE

Pictures by SYMEON SHIMIN

A SUNBURST BOOK

FARRAR, STRAUS & GIROUX · NEW YORK

DESERT

Text copyright © 1969 by Crosswicks Ltd.
Pictures copyright © 1969 by Symeon Shimin
All rights reserved
Library of Congress catalog card number: 68-29465
Published in Canada by HarperCollins*CanadaLtd*
Printed in Singapore
First edition, 1969
Sunburst edition, 1988
Third printing, 1994

Sumpta sunt vocabula, ut intellegi aliquatenus
posset quod comprehendi non porterat.

—Hugo of St Victor

DANCE IN THE DESERT

Once there was a night in the desert when nobody was afraid and everybody danced.

This was an extraordinary night, because there is terror in the desert. The man setting out with his wife and small son knew that it is not safe to cross the desert alone. He did not need to say aloud all that he knew there is to fear.

The owl screams and rushes down in a cloud of feathers and talons of steel and flies off with mouse or rabbit; the eagle snatches the straying child and bears it to a distant eyrie.

The lion, almost invisible because he is the color of sand by moonlight, stalks with snow-soft paws until he leaps upon his unsuspecting prey.

The snake slithers swiftly, tongue flickering, jeweled eyes flashing from side to side: where shall the poison strike?

There are wild asses with enormous, ludicrous, but frighteningly dangerous teeth. There are scorpions and rats and spiders.

Once, they say, a traveler was pierced through by the single horn of a unicorn. And dragons lurk in the dunes, some with wings like bats so that they can fly out at dusk upon the unwary traveler.

And then, the husband knew, there were bandits who rode across the desert on camels, their own swift-rolling pirate ships, in small, murderous bands. The only reminder of a group too weak to protect itself would be a scattering of bleached bones lying white on the golden sand. A small family could never make it alone across the burning drifts, fiercely hot from the brazen sun by day, dunes cold as snow under the moon by night.

So the parents and child, wanting to cross the desert in haste, nevertheless had to wait until they found a caravan with which they could travel. For three days caravans turned them away: the mother and child would slow them down, they said.

Therefore, the family was grateful when a rich merchant with a sizable retinue of men and beasts was willing to let them follow along.

"You must try to keep up," he said. "I have a donkey the girl can ride, and the child with her." When there were complaints from his retinue, he shrugged irritably. "What would you have me do? I have children of my own at home and it is my decision. How would I sleep at night knowing they were trying to cross the desert alone? If the baby cries too much, I will speak to its parents."

But the company learned quickly that the child was a happy little boy. He did not whine, seldom cried, and was quickly and easily distracted. He was just beginning to walk and everything delighted him: he tasted, touched, smelled, looked, listened; and rushed joyfully to show his discoveries to anybody who was willing to give him a moment's attention. During the heat of the day he slept soundly, held by his mother on the donkey. At night, when it was cooler and fires for cooking sprang up to light the sands, he was ready for play.

The desert is like the ocean. It takes time to get out of sight of land. And then suddenly there is nothing, nothing but waves of sand shifting and sliding in the wind, sand stretching out to eternity on every side. In the moonlight the fires and the tents and the camels make a small oasis for the travelers, and they draw in close, while the sands stir slowly around the caravan, spreading out into forever, and above them the stars break into distances beyond dreams.

"The child will be frightened," one of the camel drivers said, and with his great, calloused hands began to play upon a tiny reed pipe. A scrawny donkey boy ran into one of the tents and came out with an enormous horn, certainly heavier than he was, and managed to blow into it so that a braying squawk came out the end.

The little boy laughed and clapped with joy as he sat on the young man's knee in the circle around the largest of the fires.

Outside the circle, from the edges of the dark, came a deep, sustained roar. The camel driver dropped his little pipe, his huge hand reaching for his knife. "It is a lion."

The tremor of fear that ran through the group touched everybody except the child. He slid off the young man's knees and walked on his still unsteady legs to the edge of the circle.

"Wait," the mother said, as the camel driver reached for the little boy.

The firelight seemed dimmer, the moonlight on the sands outside brighter. At the crest of a dune stood a magnificent lion, completely still, so that he seemed like one of the stone carvings that the sands cover and then uncover on the desert floor. His tail began to twitch, not in anger or irritation, but in dignified rhythm.

Then, ponderously, he rose on his
hind legs to his full height. The child
stood at the edge of the circle of firelight, holding out his arms in greeting.

The lion dropped back to his four paws and moved slowly to the company, not menacing, not stalking, but in measured, courtly circles.

"He's dancing!" the donkey boy said. "The lion is dancing!"

The camel driver's grip relaxed, though he kept his hand on his knife's hilt.

At a responsible distance from the caravan the lion knelt on his forepaws, then dropped to his haunches and lay still on the sands, watching.

Again the child raised his arms in greeting, and suddenly from the dunes came a band of tiny desert mice, pink and grey, whiskers twitching in nervousness as they broke ranks and swept around the lion like a wave about a rock. They were so small that they were not even the size of the child's hand, and they leaped into the air in miniature minuet, little jet eyes flashing the moonlight. Dancing done, they, too, knelt on their forepaws in precise pattern, soft grey velvet with satin-pink noses and paws, held their obeisance for a fraction of a moment, and scurried off to wait at a safe distance from the lion.

"I have heard—" the merchant
started to say wonderingly, but stopped
as there came a great, idiotic bray, and
two enormous asses, deep grotesque
shadows, appeared, galloping in from
the horizon. Braying, they circled the
caravan once, twice, thrice, their lips
drawn back in wild and awful grins,
flopped to the sand, rolled over thrice,
their ungainly legs waving towards the
sky, then knelt, motionless, like rocks
against the dunes.

Through the stillness the child heard
and reached upwards towards the sound
of wings rushing above the caravan like
the noise of great waters or the sound
of many people crying together, and
three eagles, young and lusty, swooped
down, talons fiercely extended.

The young mother gasped, but her husband put his hand on her shoulder in a firm gesture of reassurance. "Hush. It will be all right. Do not frighten them."

"Frighten the eagles—" the merchant started angrily, then stopped as the birds arrested their flight just above the little boy, keeping aloft with a quivering of wing and tendon that made them shimmer like a mirage. They hovered there in the strange stillness of their dance under a sky fiery with stars; then the great wings beat against the air and they flew to the top of the dune above the two asses and rested there.

All eyes were on them, so that no one saw the sleek swiftness of the sliding adder until it was twined around the child's bare ankle, its scarlet tongue flickering against his tender skin like a small flame.

"Do not move," the young husband commanded as the camel driver started forward. "Be still. Then it will not harm him." His voice had a harsh authority, and the man obeyed.

The snake moved around the child's leg in sinuous swirls of affection, its undulating movements shimmering along the delicate length of its body. The child stood very still, looking down, smiling, pleased and unafraid. With a small hiss the snake dropped to the sand and slid into the shadows, where the moonlight struck against its red eyes to reveal its hiding place.

The tension of the people in the caravan was broken by the limping sound of an irregular thudding, and four ostriches, two grown birds with their young, came pounding across the desert, out of rhythm with each other, long necks stretching, bills open in greedy eagerness, heads moving foolishly from side to side. They loped up to the child, one of the young ostriches stumbling over his own splayed feet; his brother pecked at him in sibling annoyance and his father let out a reprimanding squawk; the mother ostrich looked as though she were about to bury her head in the sand. The child pealed with laughter, which was echoed throughout the caravan.

When the four great birds moved in a concerted and cumbersome tumble to their knees the little boy stopped laughing, and the guffaws of the men slowly ceased. The four birds knelt there, arrogant heads weaving, long necks curving in jerky rhythm. But the laughter was, for the moment, over. The birds fumbled to their feet and stalked across the sand.

In counterpoint to their heavy footsteps came the sound of a delicate prancing, like silver hoofs against crystal. The child looked out across the desert to the horizon, where a unicorn stood silhouetted against the path of the moon. With a toss of his head the unicorn danced lightly across the shining diamonds of sand. As he neared the circle of firelight he bowed his horned head and his flanks quivered with tension as though he were preparing to charge, but he continued lowering his horn until it touched the sand before the child in a gesture of loving reverence. Then he walked past the child to the young mother, lay down quietly beside her, and put his head in her lap. For a moment she stroked his wild mane. When she raised her hand he rose, bowed his horn once more to the child, and galloped across the desert into the path of the moon.

The silence was as shining as the
moonlight.

A flash of wings swept across the sky
and a great white bird dropped to the
sand in front of the little boy. It was a
pelican, and it had been wounded; fresh
blood stained its snowy breast feathers.
The camel driver took his knife as
though to put the bird out of its misery,
but the mother raised her hand to stop
him: there were tears in her eyes, but
she did not let them fall. The child
smiled gravely at the pelican. A drop of
blood fell from the bird's feathers onto
the sand. Bird and child looked at each
other in silence. Then the pelican turned
and walked slowly across the wilderness.

The company was becoming accustomed now to the procession of animals. A pearl-grey owl flying in the desert did not seem strange or unusual. Its eyes were ringed and wise, its beak fierce. It flew in swooping circles over the group around the fire, dipped its wings towards the child, and flew into the shadow of a dune.

The young wife turned to her husband. "The dragons and the owls honor him," she said, "because he gives waters in the wilderness, and rivers in the desert, and drink to his people." She smiled as two winged creatures, their nostrils smoking, flapped out from behind a dune. Holding their leathery wings high, they approached the edge of the circle of firelight and stood there.

The fire was flickering low and their dark wings caught only a ruddy glow from its light. Both of them slowly lowered their wings, lowered their entire bodies until they were prostrate on the sand. They backed off with clumsy reverence until they had reached the circle of animals, the lion, the mice, the wild asses, the eagles, the adder, the ostriches, the pelican, the owl: all the beasts except the unicorn had waited.

When the dragons reached them they arose, and, all together, in stern and stately pattern, they danced in a great, intricate circle around the caravan, the circle stretching, widening, until all the animals disappeared into the horizon and the birds broke loose up into the sky.

No one had noticed when the child went back to his mother, but he was in her lap, sleeping, his arms flung out, his small hands open, fingers peacefully curled. The mother's head was drooped over her child's; her arms lightly encircled him.

The stars began to dim, and at the far horizon the desert lapped against a crystal sky. Night departed. Dawn came without fear.

The camel drivers and the donkey boys prepared their animals for the next day's journey into Egypt.

The young husband led the mother and the child away from the faintly glowing coals of the fire.

The dance was over.